Reflections

Reflections

READINGS OF SPIRITUALITY, GRATITUDE, AND LOVE

Dr. Carol Kasser

Contents

IN MEMORIAM

MANNA FOR THE SOUL

DEDICATION

I wish to express my gratitude to the doctors and nurses at Fox Chase Cancer Center for their competence, caring, and compassion while I was a patient there.

In memory of Jackie, Joan, Kyle, Marlyn, and Mark, who were all taken too soon, a percentage of the royalties from this book will be donated to the Fox Chase Cancer Center and Kisses for Kyle.

For information about the **Kisses for Kyle** program, which aids young cancer patients and their families, see **www.kissesforkyle.org**

For information about the **Fox Chase Cancer Center** see **www.fccc.edu/**

Other books by Carol Kasser

Manna For the Soul: Thoughts on Religion and Spirituality
Just For Fun: Children's Poems and Stories
Diary of A Mad Camper
Stories We Brought With Us (co-author Ann Silverman)

Nature

Nature's Child

My pillow is a grassy glen,
my ceiling is the sky.
my wake-up call-a passing wren,
rustling leaves my lullaby.
My temple is the mountain,
my chapel, beneath any tree.
Each stream my drinking fountain
and God walks each step with me.

God's Canvas

The green of earth, the blue of sky,
the white of cloud wisps floating by,
the yellow daisies, lilac clover,
and wild red roses in bloom all over.
And from the rainbow color-box
God paints the mountains, seas and rocks.
Each flower, pebble, tree and fiord
is a gift hand-painted by the Lord.

God's Canvas II

Would that I could paint in words
The wondrous hues, earth greens, sky blues
that fill the universe-the canvas of the Lord.

Blue

Blue is the color of tranquility
As the lapping aqua of a gentle lake,
Or hypnotic, as the rolling blue-green of the sea,
Or magic as the powder blue sea of sky
With fluffy white gray islands all about.
How easy it is to lose myself in blue,
where rolling seas melt into sky,
and wisps of misty clouds waft by.

The Sea

I.
At dawn I love the silence
of the sea, the quiet beach,
my footprints all alone,
the caressing water lapping at my feet.
The scattered bits of wood and shells and weeds
garb the beach—and dare the sea
to come and claim them back.

II.

At noon I love the laughter
by the sea, the joyful sound
of children in the waves,
the castles all bejeweled with
stones and shells, and moats
filled with water all around.
The umbrellas and the people
deck the beach—a vast array
of colors and of shapes.

Sunset in Florence, Oregon

III.

At dusk I love the power
of the sea, the mighty waves
that lash against the rocks
and shoot into the air their salty spray.
The sea-gull dotted sky
that rivals with its
drowning, fiery rays
the majestic beauty of the wild sea.

By the Shore

I love sitting by the shore
when the sea mist enfolds me
as welcome and caressing
as your arms around me.

The Sea Breeze

The sea breeze kissed my cheek
and so did you.

Reflections at Crater Lake

I.

Mount Mazama blew its top
and left a perfect bowl;
cragged rocks all around,
inside an empty hole.
Rain and snow filled the gap,
Slowly, over time
And made a lake blue, so blue,
cold, clear, sublime.
Rocky little isles formed.
Thus Mount Mazama said,
"I may reclaim this lake one day;
I'm sleeping, but not dead."

II.

Hillsides reflect in water so clear;
where does mountain end and image begin?

III.

The floating trunk, an oddity,
bobs upright like a cork,
playing peek-a-boo about the lake,
daring tourist boats to find it.

The lake water is cold and pure
from rain and snow created,
and waterfalls like daring boys
dive down into the blue.

IV.
Aqua, azure, midnight
So purely, clearly, blue
I can tell the varied depths
by the surface's changing hue.

Family Love

Daddy Came Home

Daddy came home, daddy came home!
I smell the pancakes he always makes me
when he is home on Sunday morning.
I run barefoot down the steps,
skid across the cold, green floor.
The pancakes are already stacked;
the checkered cloth on the big oak table,
and dad sits on the hard brown chair.
I hop up on his lap, and I, too, am home.
I see his ever-present coffee there.
For me, he makes it ecru and not tan.
I hear the ice cubes clinking in his glass.
"Don't let your mother see. Here take a sip."
That memory now is as bittersweet
as that coffee on my lips.
Daddy came home. But he couldn't stay.

Teenage Love

When I was fourteen and in love with you,
our folks called it passing fancy,
but you and I knew better.
You made me grow to like myself,
to accept my abilities-and limitations,
to accept life and enjoy it.
At fourteen I knew that which many people never learn.
You taught me compassion, love, and understanding.
And when I was seventeen, and my parents divorced,
you taught me to forgive unintentional pain.
Now when I look back on those bittersweet years,
I know that the *me* I am today
was shaped by the *you* of my teenage years.

The Marriage Quilt

A marriage is like a fine quilt. The squares of the marriage quilt are trust, honesty, respect, fidelity, appreciation, laughter, forgiveness, shared interests, understanding, friendship, compromise, faith, and common values. And love is the thread that binds it together.

Break even one strand and there is a tear in the fabric of the marriage. Repair any damage quickly or the marriage quilt may begin to unravel.

But treat the quilt gently, watch the squares and threads for even the slightest signs of wear, and mend any tears quickly, and your marriage quilt will keep you warm, safe and secure for a lifetime.

Across Generations

I accept your right to your own beliefs and actions-
as long as they hurt no one.
I ask only that you act always in faith with your conscience
and values.
I do not ask you to live in accordance with mine.
Your beliefs are the product of your experience and time
and my values are the result of mine.
If we have a common ground, it is because I am part of the
experience that shaped your life, and you have examined my ideals
and found some of them worthwhile for you.
That is all I ask of you—to study the beliefs you see around you
and accept those that are right for you—
then strive always to make your actions match your ideals.
I will not force my thoughts on you—you have your own.
I will not ask you to live by my ideals-you are not me,
but I do expect you to live up to your own.
And I ask the same of you-that you judge me not by how well
I've lived up to your expectations and beliefs,
but by how well I've lived by mine.

Impatient Mother's Prayer

For just one day let me not say
"Go away, leave me alone,
shut up, I don't care."
Let me not say "no" when I could say "yes"

or worse-when I never even heard the question.
For just today let me not yell when I can talk,
blame when I can praise.
Let me tell them what they've done right
not what they've done wrong.
Just today, I want to thank them
for the errands they remembered
instead of scolding for what they forgot.
Just for today let me ask instead of order,
request and not demand.
For this one time let me speak to them and listen
with respect for their opinions
as I would with my friends.
For just today I will find and praise their strengths,
not see and criticize their faults.
And just perhaps they will learn that I love them.
And just maybe they will learn to love themselves.

To Harris

How can I be with another
when you are nestled in my heart?
You are there when we are together,
and still there when we are apart.
I can feel what you are feeling
and know what you want to say.
You're a scene in each dream I'm dreaming
And a verse in each prayer I pray.
There's nowhere that I could travel,
and no place where you could be
that I wouldn't feel you beside me.
You've become a part of me.

I Love
crunching autumn leaves
walks in the rain
the sea breeze
sunshine
YOU!

Gratitude of an Adopted Child

How different my life could have been
if you hadn't chosen to take me in;
if you hadn't taught me to believe
that anything I dreamed of, I could achieve.
If my early years hadn't been full of
family, friends, unconditional love.
How many with potential bright as mine
were never given a chance to shine?
Whatever I am, whatever I do,
is only possible because of you.

To The Woman Who Bore Me

To the woman who bore me and let me go
it was an act of love, I know.
You had no money; you weren't a wife.
You wanted to give me a chance in life.
I've had the life you wished for me;
I've had love, family, opportunity.
If you've ever questioned what you had to do,
You made the right choice; I'm grateful to you.

Drifting Apart

When we were teenagers in love
the world conspired to pull you away.
But we trusted our love and clung to each other
and celebrated our wedding day.
Through family divorces and deaths,
Through children and pets, we shared our hearts.
Then, sadly, one day we stopped clinging,
and we simply   drifted   apart.

Bubbe

A weathered face, and gray-white hair,
a slackened step, and dimming eyes,
the world looks at you, and that is what it sees.
But I look in your eyes, and I see you.
I see eighty years of loving and being loved.

I see patience and courage, strength and wit.
I see wisdom, humor, joy and sorrow.
I sense the yearning to learn and work and do
that keeps you ever young.
Your eighty tears have aged you,
but they have not made you old.

Bubbe's House

Cinnamon sticks and camphor balls
And simmering lamb stew
The smells of love and comfort,
The aromas of Bubbe's house.

Bubbe Sarah and great granddaughter Stacy
Photo by Judie Ford

I Look Too Old

Bubbe Sarah is eighty-eight years old. I have a picture of her holding my four-year-old daughter. The way they were looking at each other just emanated mutual love right out of the picture. But when I showed the picture to Bubbe, her only comment was, "I don't like it. It makes me look too old!"

I Can't Hear

Bubbe Sarah was at lunch with her friends Sadie and Rose. Sadie sat on Bubbe's left and kvetched about her kids, her health, her late husband. Bubbe never said a word. Finally, Rose nudged her and said, "Sarah, Sadie is talking to you." "Oh," Bubbe replied, "I guess my hearing in that ear isn't as good as it used to be."

Several weeks later the friends were having lunch again. This time Sadie sat on Bubbe's right. Again Sadie bemoaned her life, her health, her family, and again Bubbe said nothing. Once more Rose nudged her and said "Sarah, Sadie is talking to you." Again Bubbe said, "Oh I'm sorry. I guess my hearing in that ear isn't as good as it used to be."

Later that day, Rose approached her. "I'm worried about your hearing. Maybe you should see a doctor. But I don't understand it. You always seem to hear me perfectly." "Yes," said Bubbe with a smile, "It's funny how the hearing comes and goes depending on the topic of conversation."

Stacy

Four-year-old Stacy was playing cards with her older brother and sister. Her dad was curious to see if she knew what she was doing, so he asked to see her hand. She smiled, put down her cards, and held up her palm.

Four-year-old Stacy idolized her seven-year-old twin brother and sister. One day the older two were discussing what they want to be when they grow up. Finally I turned to Stacy and asked what she wanted to be when she grew up. She promptly answered, "Seven."

It was Stacy's fifth birthday. We celebrated with the obligatory party with presents, cake balloons and friends. Then ever the tomboy, she changed out of her party clothes and ran outside to play soccer with her friends. About an hour later she ran in all excited and breathless, waving a twenty-dollar bill. "Look what I found on the front lawn, Mom. I think it's my birthday present from God."

We were on a cross-country trip when we stopped at the Grand Canyon. We went into the cafeteria where Stacy bought some apple pie. As she was about to bite into it, she noticed some strange, white fuzz on it. "Look, Mom, she laughed, "It's pie a la mold."

Sam and Rose

Poppop Sam and Nanny Rose seemed to have a good marriage. I often wondered how he managed to maintain his calm when she began to nag or scold. Then one day, it all became clear. She came into the room and began to harangue him about some errands she wanted done. He winked at me as he turned off his hearing aid. Then he turned to her, smiled and nodded.

Readings for a Daughter and her Unborn Child

My Baby's having a Baby

My Baby is Having A Baby

My baby is having a baby.
How can it be?
I look at her and see ringlet curls, tutus,
balance beams and soccer balls.
I see the three-year-old reading **Hop on Pop**
and writing her first card, albeit backwards,
and finger-painting lovely pastel masterpieces.
My baby is having a baby.
When did she become this charming woman,
strong, bright, determined, loving?
Soon her world will fill
with baby steps and curly hair
and gym mats and soccer balls
and nursery rhymes and Dr. Seuss
and scribbled, painted works of love.
My baby is having a baby,
                    . . . lucky baby.

To My Pregnant Daughter

I watch your body swelling,
growing with new life.
I look at you, my daughter,
now a woman and a wife.
You've filled my life with love,
with blessing and with pride.
I wish for you the same joy
from the child who grows inside.
Savor every moment
of this blessing of your own.
Children are a wondrous gift-
But they're much too quickly grown.

To My Daughter

I loved you from the moment that
I knew that you would be,
and treasured the months I felt you
growing inside of me.
I loved you from the moment
I first held you in my arms,
and the early years of learning
your moods, your ways, your charms.
I loved the discovery years
when everything was new.
I learned to see the world again
through the eyes of you.
I loved you through the school years
when you grew in body and in mind,
and your character began to form,
bright, athletic, kind.
I even loved the teenage years
when you were struggling to see
how to become the young adult
that you were meant to be.
Now I love your adult years.

You've become the perfect blend
of love, of strength and gentleness,
my child and my friend.
Most of all I love this time
as the cycle of life renews,
and you begin to love this life
that grows inside of you.

A Prayer for an Unborn Child

Please God,
Keep this baby safe and whole
In body, mind, spirit, soul.
Give it kindness, wisdom, health,
love and patience, strength and wealth.
Complete acceptance, unconditional love,
and faith in Your guidance from above.

I Saw a Miracle Today

I saw a miracle today.
Just centimeters long, but a miracle nonetheless,
a living, growing wonder, with a beating heart,
a tiny head, and newly forming body,
God's miracle in progress,
Heaven's gift in the process of becoming.
I saw creation right before my eyes
in a sonogram of my unborn grandchild.
Thank You, God, I saw a miracle today.

To My Daughter on Giving Me a Grandchild

I thought that mother love
was the best love that could be.
I treasured the gifts of joy and hope
that you have brought to me.
But when I held your child
who melted into my heart,
I found that there's another love,
even deeper and apart.

New Baby

Every day is a joy,
every day's a surprise
when I look at the world
through your wondrous eyes.

Dear Baby,

What an amazing world you will come to: A world of cars, planes, e-mail, computers, space ships, camcorders, genetic engineering, a world of unlimited possibilities. Learn to be part of the hi-tech world but stay firmly grounded in humanity. Strive for your future but don't forget your past.

Dear Baby,

I

Grow wings . . . and roots, which is my way of saying know when to reach for the stars and when to keep your feet planted firmly on the ground.

II

I hope you see the miracles in the world around you . . .
and know that you are one of them.
See the holy in yourself . . . and in others.
See endless love in the wagging tail of a puppy . . .
and in my eyes.

III

Treat others as you wish to be treated.
Forgive meanness, remember kindness.
Allow yourself to express your feelings.
Cry when you must, laugh when you can,
And love unconditionally.
Choose peace,
Choose tolerance,
Choose understanding,
Choose love.

IV
Remember that you can't control every situation,
but you can control your reaction to it.
Respect yourself . . . and others.
Remember that I love you . . .
And remember to love yourself.
Know that the world is God's gift to you . . .
and you are God's gift to the world.
Use God's gifts wisely.

To My Granddaughter

I wish you beauty and grace, inside and out.
I wish you strength. I wish you love and joy. I wish you courage and
gentleness and faith.
Dare to take chances!
Dare to believe
anything you strive for,
you can achieve.
Never let others undermine your faith in yourself.
Never let others guide you against the promptings of your own
conscience. Do for others when you can, but don't bury your own
needs. Get a good moral foundation and then make sure your actions
are always guided by it. Know you are loved; love yourself; love others.
Don't let others place limitations on you. Never heed the words "You
can't. You're a girl." Believe you can *because* you are a girl. Don't believe
that being loved makes you a worthwhile person. Know that you are a
worthwhile person, and love will find you. Love is what matters. And
as long as I am in this world, and even after I pass into the next, never
ever doubt that you are loved.

To My Grandchild

Long after I am gone, a thread of my life will go on in you. I love you
for yourself, for who you are. And I love you for what you are to me,
my heart, my soul, my immortality.

Making Memories

Collecting shell or jumping waves,
building castles by the sea,

sharing our time out in the sun,
we are creating a memory.
When making little paper kites
and flying them in the breeze,
or tossing a baseball back and forth,
we are making new memories.
Gathering leaves and acorns,
swinging in a tire on a tree,
picnicking under the old elm,
we are building a memory.
And when I am old, or not here at all,
if you sometimes think of me,
I hope you will joyously recall
how we created each memory.

Pets Are Family, Too

Cuddle and Tuffy
It's nice to have someone to snuggle with

Life Lesson I learned from my Cat

1.   It's nice to have someone to snuggle with.
2.   Everyone needs unconditional love.
3.   Humans aren't God's only intelligent creations.
4.   Cats are creative thinkers.
5.   Stake out your own turf in life.
6.   Keep an adventurous spirit.
7.   It's good for the soul to have someone purr in your ear.
8.   Admire agility, grace and beauty wherever they are found.
9.   Cooperate-you scratch my back; I'll scratch yours.
10. There's nothing better to raise your spirits than something little, soft, and loving sitting in your lap.
11. Nap often!
12. Stretch when you get up.
13. Schedule playtime into your daily life.
14. Age gracefully.
15. Trust animals' intuition and instincts.
16. Always land on your feet.
17. Any problem can be solved with creative thinking and persistent effort.

18. Like people, animals have unique, individual personalities.
19. Healthy curiosity is a good thing.
20. If cleanliness is next to Godliness, expect to see kittens at the foot of God's throne.
21. Keep yourself clean and well-groomed.
22. Cats are always there when you need them.
23. Don't take yourself too seriously.
24. Today's newspaper headliner is tomorrow's litter box liner.
25. Aim high!
26. When you see an opportunity, pounce on it.
27. Be independent!
28. Cats are a humbling influence. No matter how rich and powerful you are, your cat still won't listen to you!
29. Be a leader, not a follower.
30. Have close friends.
31. But also learn to amuse yourself.
32. Blind obedience isn't a virtue.
33. If you like to be in control, don't get a cat.
34. Any person can be cat-broken.
35. Tell a cat where he cannot go, and he'll find a way to get there.
36. It is possible to be strong and gentle at the same time.
37. Socialize, but also be comfortable by yourself.
38. If you claw your way to the top, those wearing your claw marks won't forget on your way back down.
39. Cats' cries have as many different meanings as babies' cries- and a real cat lover can distinguish among them.
40. It is possible to live-and die—with dignity.
41. Animals mourn.
42. Human loss is not the only loss worth mourning.
43. Hugging a cat really helps ease pain.
44. Everyone needs to find a place in the sun.

My Cuddles

Cuddles was dark gray and white. He was the cat equivalent of a mutt, although his green almond-shaped eyes and his sly intelligence hinted at Siamese in his family tree. He was an indoor cat, a people lover who lived up to his name.

But somewhere in his veins ran the blood of his wild forebears. Once in a while this lovable, huggable, docile fur ball would get the urge for adventure, for a day of stalking in the woods like his noble ancestors. On those days, when I opened the door, a flash of gray would tear past me, down the hill behind our house, and into the woods. Later in the evening, dirty, tired, hungry and cold, but self-satisfied, he'd show up at the door. Stoically, he'd submit to the washing, powdering, scolding and pampering that greeted his return.

On one such cold, crisp winter day, he bolted out the door and headed for adventure. But this day, he got more than he bargained for.

His feral ancestors would have known by the gray sky and the bite in the air, that this was a day to take cover. But he was much too excited by his freedom to note such details.

Late in the afternoon, not rain, not even snow, but ice, sleet and frozen rain pelted the area. Evening came. We called for him. We looked for him. No Cuddles!

Morning came, a crisp breath-taking morning. Trees glimmered like diamonds, their boughs bent beneath the weight of their coats of shimmering ice. Schools closed; offices closed. The streets were skating rinks.

My husband Harris, clad in parka, boots and gloves walked, slid, skidded around the house, the yard, the neighborhood, calling for Cuddles. Finally he heard a pathetic "mew" from the woods at the bottom of the hill behind the house. "Cuddles," my husband called. The shivering wet fur ball took a few tentative steps up the icy hill and slid back down. Again he tried, and slid back down. He sat there wet and cold, mewing pathetically.

Harris decided that he had to rescue the cat. I had visions of him slipping down the hill and squashing Cuddles. I could picture broken hips and rescue squads coming to save them both.

But that was his baby down there, and Harris was going to save him. Like Tarzan swinging through the trees, Harris slid from one frozen tree branch to another. I prayed that the frozen branches wouldn't snap off in his hands. Triumphantly, he reached the bottom, scooped up the half-frozen cat-sicle, and zipped him into the parka. With the cold, frightened cat squirming inside his coat, Harris crawled back up the hill, grasping onto tree branch after tree branch. Often he'd creep up two feet and slide back one. Finally man and cat arrived home safely. The cat was wrapped in blankets, fed and pampered. The man was scolded for risking his fool neck.

After that experience, even when Cuddles was just going out onto the balcony, before he would venture out, he would glance up furtively at the sky!

Cuddles—He had been known to try to stow away in an open suitcase

Cuddles: In Memoriam by Harris Biegelman

Cuddles, an alley cat, had been with us for more than sixteen years. Early in his life he established that he was going to be in charge of his destiny. When he was fed what he did not approve of, he placed his paw under his plate and hurled it at my shin. To his human family, he more than lived up to the name Cuddles. He was always available for petting, for having his tummy rubbed, and for bonding with all those who showed him affection. Most mornings before feeding, he would let me pick him up and he would place his paws around my neck and purr to me.

He expected an early breakfast meal prepared by me. On a day that I decided to sleep late, his roused his "brother" Tuffy, placed him next to our door, then placed his body next to Tuffy's. And with their two bodies swinging in unison, they banged on the door to open it.

To those who did not acknowledge his presence he was most annoyed. We had a house guest who ignored him, preferring to read in bed before retiring. Cuddles leapt from the hallway onto the bed and peed on the covers to let the guest know not to ignore him. Even

Carol was not immune. When she was busy typing on her computer, ignoring the cat, Cuddles went to the surge protector, and with a flip of the paw, turned the computer off.

In every respect, Cuddles was a family member. He was more than that. He was a true pal. When we came in, he greeted us. When he wished to be alone, he would retreat to his control center under the dining room table, where no one could touch him, but where he could watch everything to be sure that it was to his liking.

An example of his acuity was when he was locked into a room, he knew to turn the doorknob. He stretched up for it, but couldn't quite reach it. "They don't make these for cats," he mused. In succession he plotted several options, placed them in priority sequence and executed each alternative until he achieved his goal. Not too many people use thinking skills that well.

Cuddles may have been the best non-human fan of Johnny Carson. Every night, just past 11:30 when the Tonight Show theme song came on, Cuddles leapt onto our bed, pointed his ears at the TV and watched the show. When the show started five minutes later, Cuddles waited the extra five minutes to appear on our bed. When extended sports or news delayed the show, Cuddles delayed his entry.

I had been in the hospital for an operation. Carol was with me all day. When I came home and went to bed, as first cat, Cuddles knew his place was beside me. He sat by me, tending to my emotional needs.

He enjoyed having Carol and me around, even if it was just to ignore us. When I put on my shoes, he was upset, because it meant I was going out for a time and would not be there to frolic with him.

We had to hide suitcases from his brother and him. He knew that a suitcase meant that we were going away overnight, and he would have to stay alone with his brother. He had been known to try to stow away in an open suitcase.

When we came back, he would hide from us to show his displeasure. I would find him, pick him up, and then he would purr to show that he forgave me, and to show that he was glad that we were back to share the joy of life with him.

When we got a new reclining chair, he approved. He jumped into the chair, spread his paws out, flipped his tail, and relaxed completely. As he was about to fall asleep, he gave us a look that said, "I hope you get one just like this for yourselves. This one's for me."

Carol and I had planned a six day trip. When Cuddles saw that we were rolling out the suitcases, he and his brother were visibly upset. He was going to miss us. We left plenty of food and water and even hired a cat-sitter to visit and play with them twice a day.

On our return, Cuddles looked underweight. Our cat-sitter reported that he was drinking excessively, but refused to eat. At first, I attributed this to his missing us. When he did not respond to feeding, Carol and I took him to the vet. She said that Cuddles had kidney failure and that it was a matter of time.

Cuddles was growing weaker. By hand, I fed him dietary supplements and I gave him vitamin C and liquid A for his kidney. I had to put water into him with a medicine dropper. Nothing helped. He hadn't purred in days. I picked him up. He put his limp paws around my neck. "For you, I will purr in your ear one last time," he seemed to say to me. At night his brother would sit by his side. I think they were reminiscing about all the good times they had together.

A morning came when Cuddles had not moved; he did not take in any water. He couldn't leave his bed, not even to go to the bathroom. We cried for our clean, proud cat who had sat all night in a wet bed. We all knew it was time to let him go. "I do not want you to feel bad," he said with his eyes. "I'm just tired out."

Stacy, his mommy, came to see him for the last time. Before we left the house with him for the last time, Stacy told Tuffy to say goodbye to his brother. Tuffy walked over as if he understood. He sat down in front of Cuddles and for a few silent moments, the two just looked at each other. There wasn't a dry eye in the house.

We took Cuddles to Stacy's house, the place where he had grown up. He was placed on the lawn, still in his bed. His former neighbors came to visit him, to pet him, to be with him. With the last strength that was in him, he held his head high, felt the breeze on his face, and smelled the flowers. He seemed to say, "I enjoyed this lawn; I romped here. This is a beautiful warm breezy, sunny day. I do not want any of you to be sad. I am happy that you have come to be with me. I have had a good life."

His mommy picked him up one last time and we took him to the vet. He left us.

When we arrived home, Tuffy looked for Cuddles. Now he

understood. Tuffy sat in the very spot where Cuddles' bed had been and yowled in grief.

We moved Tuffy's bed to the spot where Cuddles had slept. He refused to get into it until we moved it back. He would not take his brother's place. For weeks, every once in a while Tuffy would emit a heart-wrenching howl. We knew he was thinking of Cuddles. Finally, a year later, to the day, Tuffy had a stroke. He would be lonely no longer. He joined Cuddles.

In Memory of Cuddles 10/4/00 by Carol Kasser

I can put roses on the table now
since he's not here to eat them.
But when my feet are cold at night,
he isn't there to heat them.
He had a funny, furry way
of getting to my soul.
He brought me love and laughter,
and made the world seem whole.
Now my house is quieter,
and now it's odor-free,
but I'd gladly take back the mess
to have the joy he brought to me.
I can sleep much later now.
No cat's purring at my door.
And that job I hate, the litter box,
isn't a problem any more.
But the quiet house is deafening.
I miss his impish charms.
I'd gladly clean and brush and feed,
to hold him purring in my arms.

My Faith

Thanksgiving
Thank God for leaves of red

Thanksgiving

Thank you God for leaves of red,
for white clouds floating overhead.
Thank you God for babies small,
and for your blessings over all,
for purple azaleas in the spring.
Thank you God for everything.
For ocean's waves and fresh salt air,
and snowflakes falling everywhere.
For summer breezes softly blowing,
and happy children when it's snowing.
For life, and health, for friends and love,
for watching over us from above.
For babies' cooing and birds that sing,
thank you God for everything.

Banff
Waterfalls cascading down

Banff

If there's a heaven I hope it looks like Banff.
It's impossible to see this place
and not know that God is.
In awe, staring up at snow-capped mountains,
and waterfalls cascading down,
I know The Rock of Ages.
Looking up at the trees and rocks
swept down by an avalanche,
I know the meaning of The Almighty.
Standing in the rarified air of a mountain peak,
looking down on lakes and trees, and clouds,
I understand the words Most High.
Stepping out on a glacier,
walking on ice 40,000 years old,

I come to know The Eternal.
I may not yet find here a lion lying down with a lamb,
but in this place where no hunting is allowed,
I have seen moose, bears, wolves, and mountain goats
so close that I could touch them,
living in harmony with man.
Here I have tasted the promise of The World to Come.
In rushing rivers and cascading falls,
I find meaning to The Source of All.
In the lush green trees and darting squirrels,
I see the reality of the Living God.
I find here not only the creations,
but also the Holy source of all, the Creator.

Where is God?

I see God in the clouds above.
I see God in a tree.
I find God in a yellow rose.
I feel God inside of me.
I hear God in the ocean's roar.
I sense God in the air.
I feel God in a passing breeze.
God's works are everywhere.
I smell God in the lilac bush,
touch God in a baby's face.
I hear God in a singing bird.
God's love is every place.

Israel

After the ashes of carnage,
Amidst hatred and fear,
surrounded by enemy nations
who swore to make us disappear,
in 1948, tiny Israel was born.
More than half a century later
Surviving war year after year
To friends and foes we declare out loud
Despite all, we're still here.

Holocaust Remembrance Day

The day to remember relatives I can never meet,
cousins who were never born,
friendships and loves that never had a chance
to blossom and to grow.
I mourn six million, and more, so many more,
all the children and grandchildren
who never came to be;
I mourn them all.
I mourn the loss of innocence,
of faith in the basic goodness of humanity,
of faith even in the Almighty,
among those that blame God
and not man for those awful days.
I mourn for the guilt and the pain of the survivors,
and I mourn for myself-that I will never feel
completely secure anywhere because of what has been.
And yet in the depths of the mourning,
there is still a seed of hope.
Remembering those righteous ones
who risked their lives to help,
I have hope that someday all humanity
will view each other as family,
as children of the same God,
and all will choose to be their brother's keepers.
There is hope in the survival of the Jewish people
and humanity despite all efforts at destruction.
There is hope in the existence of Israel
reborn from the ashes of the Shoah.
There is sorrow in remembering the past,
but it must be remembered
so that it may never be repeated.
But as always with the Jewish people,
Even in this sorrow and despair,
there is still tikvah, hope.
*shoah-holocaust
tikvah-hope

Happiness

```
      P I N
  P       E
 A         S
H           S
```

Is like a rainbow
Always in sight
But try thought you might
                You
                    Can't
                        Reach
                            It!
I wrote that as a teenager.
Now I know it isn't true.
Joy isn't found externally.
It starts inside of you.

To God

I praise you in the morning light;
before I go to sleep at night.
I feel your awe in earth and sky,
in wispy white clouds wafting by,
In rushing rivers, tall oak trees,
twinkling stars and fragrant breeze.
I hear you in a cat's meow,
and in a newborn baby's howl.
I see your light in children's eyes.
I hear your whisper in old men's sighs.
So I praise you in the morning sun,
and then again when day is done.

My God

I know You by the world You've made,
sun for light and trees for shade.
I see You in a starry night.
I feel Your warmth in firelight.
I see You in a sky of blue.

I hear You in a baby's coo.
I feel You in my grandson's smile,
and when I sit by the sea awhile.
I feel You in my husband's hug.
I see You in a ladybug.
I smell You in a fragrant flower.
I touch You in a light sun shower.
I taste You in a sip of wine.
I feel You in the bright sunshine.
I know You by the world You've wrought,
by the lessons that Your Book has taught.
So day by day Your praise I sing:
Thank you God for everything.

These things bring joy
Red azaleas ablaze on a hill

These Things Bring Joy

The sparkle in a child's eyes,
Dark nights lit by fireflies,
A newborn baby's first sweet cries,
These things make my heart arise.
Water rippling o'er rocks in a rill,
Red azaleas ablaze on a hill,
Autumn evenings crisp and still,
These things help my soul to fill.

Fluffy clouds afloat in space,
A smile on a weathered face,
Squirrels scurrying from place to place,
These bring moments of quiet grace.

Let My Life Be My Prayer

When my voice cannot, let my life sing to You,
a song of faith, of joy, of love,
of gratitude, compassion, caring, hope.
When the words or the voice fail me,
let my life stand before You as my prayer.

A Breathing Meditation for Healing

Breathe in healing, breathe out fear.
Breathe in peace, breathe out pain.
Breathe in love, breathe out anger.
Breathe in forgiveness, breathe out grudges.
Breathe in comfort, breathe out sorrow.
Breathe in serenity, breathe out stress.
Breathe in healing, breathe out fear.
Breathe in peace, breathe out pain.

Here's to the Lonely

Here's to the lonely, the forgotten, the ill.
God loved them always, God loves them still.
For those who feel friendless, for those who might cry,
"No one will care if I live or I die."
This I am sure of, this they should know,
There's a special place in heaven for those ignored down below.

The Grand Canyon

Havdalah at the Grand Canyon

It was Saturday evening, almost time for Havdalah service, but our family had no Havdalah set with us as we stood at Hopi Point in the Grand Canyon.

We whispered a prayer, "Blessed are You Creator of the Universe who separates between dark and light, between holy and profane, between Sabbath and the other six days of the week."

No wine cup was available, so we drank in the beauty of the canyon. There was no braided candle, so we focused our eyes on the last burning rays of sunlight as they were extinguished behind the majestic mountain peaks.

There was no spice box, but we inhaled the fragrance of the surrounding pines, and we could feel the tranquility and the awe inspired by this day and this scene, accompany us into the new week.

An unusual service? Certainly! But it was the most memorable Havdalah we have ever experienced.

Havdalah: A ceremony on Saturday night marking the end of the Jewish Sabbath and the beginning of the week.

A Meditation Retreat

"A five-day meditation retreat for clergy," I read. "Well, why not?" I thought. It was the week after Passover, and as a Jewish geriatric Chaplain, Passover was a notoriously hectic week for me. So I headed up to the Catskill Mountains of New York.

After a nerve-wracking five hour drive, I arrived. Before I even checked in, I took a look at the itinerary for the retreat.

Item #1 for Monday's schedule was **5:45 a.m.: Wake up.** They're kidding, right? I came up here for rest and relaxation. I looked at the rest of the schedule.

6:15 Sit Sit? I'm getting up at 5:45 to sit? I'm a doer not a sitter!

7:00 Personal Practice (private prayers) Fine! I'd be doing that at home anyway.

8:00 Breakfast Okay. Finally something I can look forward to. But wait. This place is known for food that is healthy, kosher, and vegetarian. I am a carnivore who thinks chocolate is a basic food group. I perused the rest of the itinerary.

9:00 Sit

9:45 Walk

10:30 Sit

11:15 Walk

12:00 Sit

12:30 Lunch

The schedule for the afternoon was much the same. This wasn't my idea of a vacation, but what the heck, I was already here.

It was already late Sunday afternoon when I checked in. I dragged my suitcase (I never had learned the art of packing lightly) up a hill, up a flight of steps and to my room. Accommodations were Spartan, but adequate. Each room was part of a mini-suite, emphasis on mini, with an entryway, a shared bath, and two tiny bedrooms. My bedroom had two single beds, a nightstand and lamp, and a cubby-remember cubbies from day camp? I was worried about that other bed. The room was the size of my walk-in closet at home. Would there be another person in this miniscule room? My other concern was the shared bathroom. I'm 53 years old. I don't have a sharing-the-bathroom kind of bladder. I was relieved to learn that although there was someone in the other room of the mini-suite, each little cell would be private.

We gathered for dinner: Homemade lentil soup, salad bar, fresh fruit tray, assorted breads including pumpernickel raison, my favorite in the world. The salmon cakes (good it isn't totally vegetarian) were delicious. No soda, but herbal teas and fruit juices and water.

After dinner we went downstairs to the meditation room. The leaders, Sylvia Boorstein, Sheila Peltz, and Jeff Roth, began to explain the program. I heard them explain that meditation calms the mind and body. It leads to peace, tranquility, mindfulness, expansiveness of soul, compassion, patience, discipline, and impulse control. Uh oh! They lost me on those last three! For the past five years on Yom Kippur, patience and food control (that would be impulse control) were always at the top of the list of things I'd pray for in the coming year. I was not only impulsive; in some aspects of my life, eating and shopping among them, I was borderline compulsive!

As the leaders talked, they established some ground rules for the retreat. There were no telephones, alarm clocks, radios or televisions in the rooms. We were not to use cell phones, computers or beepers. They preferred that we not read or write. Except for scheduled lectures and question and answer periods, there was to be no talking. "Okay," I thought "I'm out of here! When's the next train? Oh right, I drove and it's night-time. I have night blindness. I guess I'm staying."

We had out first meditation "sit." We were told to focus on our breathing. For me that was anxiety-producing, not calming. I had always taken breathing for granted until the previous summer when I had developed asthma. Focusing on my breathing, I flashed back to earlier months when I couldn't draw a deep breath, when I couldn't catch my breath. We had been told in the "sit" to push all other thoughts away, to stay in the moment, to focus on the breaths. I tried again. The thoughts came back again. I did not have a good "sit."

At 9:30, meditation was over. I went to my room and was asleep by 10:00.

Day 2 I rose at 5:45, awakened by a bell that sounded like a wind chime. If one has to get up at 5:45, the chime is a pleasant sound to wake to.

I stumbled bleary-eyed into the meditation room at 6:15. I still wasn't comfortable focusing on my breaths, but I managed to stay focused for about 15 minutes. Then I started to squirm in my seat. Itches and aches arose unbidden. I scratched. I moved. Another 15 minutes crept by. I peeked open my eyes. My colleagues sat silent, still, eyes closed, some on chairs, some cross-legged on prayer pillows on the floor. Everyone seemed to be tranquil. Why couldn't I be? I closed my eyes. I tried focusing on my breathing, but it was impossible. My mind would not stay calm. Neither would my body. "If this doesn't end soon," I thought, "I will scream." At long last I heard the little chime that signaled the end of the "sit." I fairly jumped out of my chair and rushed up the steps.

We had an hour for prayers before breakfast. That I could do. That was part of my daily routine anyway.

8:00 a.m. Breakfast! It was strange eating in silence, avoiding eye contact. But the food was wonderful. Pumpernickel with raisons, healthy cereals, oatmeal, yogurt, fresh fruit, some egg-custard dish that wasn't quite flan and wasn't quite kugel, but it was quite delicious.

9:00 a.m. Uh oh! Time to "sit" again! Before the sit came a brief comment from the instructors. "Some of you need to work on impulse control. If you have an itch, don't automatically scratch it. Focus on the spot and continue to breathe slowly; the same for slight aches and pains. Stay still and breathe unless is so bad that it affects your concentration."

Am I paranoid, or was he looking directly at me when he gave those instructions? I really tried this time. I even sat on a pillow on the floor. I breathed. My ankles ached. For some reason they were very swollen. I didn't move (much), but I didn't focus either. I couldn't focus on my breathing. It reminded me of my asthma. I tried to focus on my body. My mind raced off to all the ways my body had betrayed me in the past year-developing asthma, chronic sinusitis, bronchitis, migraine headaches, endometrial cancer. I tried to calm my mind and breathe. A few moments of focus, and then my mind wandered off again. It suddenly dawned on me that my mind and my body were at war. All of my life, my body had done what my mind asked it to do, and my mind had made some pretty extraordinary demands. Climb Mount Fuji! Do a 60+ mile bike-a-thon to Atlantic City! Do a mini-triathlon! Walk the Dublin Marathon! That last request had come a scant three years before, just prior to my 50th birthday when I already weighed over 200 pounds. My mind asked; my body obeyed . . . until this year when my body betrayed me with illness and weakness. I asked it to train for a mini-triathlon again, and it responded with swollen ankles and shortness of breath. I realized my mind was racing again, not relaxed, not focused.

At last the sit was over and we had question and answer time. I raised my hand. "This isn't working for me. You ask me to focus on my breathing, but that reminds me that I have asthma. You ask me to focus on my body, but my body betrayed me this year. My mind and my body are at war. 'In my body' is the last place I want to be right now. I have done meditation before. It is what got me through the weeks before, during and after surgery. But it was guided meditation in which I focused on something external and comforting, a flickering candle, a prayer, the sounds of a mini-waterfall, the vision of a peaceful place, pictures of my children and grandchildren. That worked for me precisely because it took my focus away from my body. How am I supposed to do this type of meditation?"

The answer was "There are two types of meditation. The guided meditation serves an important purpose, but so does this kind. It calms the body and mind. It brings you to a place of peace and expansiveness of soul that allows you to see things more clearly. You don't have to focus on your breath or your body, but you have to focus on something that exists in the moment." Just then a bird began singing outside the window. "You could focus on the sound of the bird. That is in the moment."

We left with instructions for our walk. "Remember the walk is not a break. It is another opportunity to focus. The purpose is not to take a walk. It is to focus on the process of walking. Focus on your steps as you walk. How you lift your leg. How you put your foot down."

I tried to focus on my feet as I walked and became painfully aware that they were swollen and sore. "This isn't going well, either," I thought. I walked a block and came to a little rill with water rippling over some rocks. The sound of water, my favorite sound! I could focus on that. It kept me in the moment and it relaxed me. I walked back and forth in a small area that kept me in earshot of the water. I felt the cold, crisp air on my face. I heard the rippling water. And suddenly, with startling clarity, a thought came to me. My mind and my body were at war, but they didn't need to be. All my life my body had acceded to the wishes of my mind. Now it was time to redefine the relationship. At least for now, my mind would have to adjust to the limitations of my body. Like that, in an instant, the war was over. For the first time in nearly a year, I felt at home in my body. I walked back peacefully for the next sit.

I sat on a chair this time, since the earlier sit on the floor had left my legs in agony. I found that I could focus on my breath without my mind rebelling and racing away. I sat in focused silence. Finally I peeked at my watch. 20 minutes! Not bad! I still didn't remain motionless for the rest of the sit. I put my head in my hands for the remainder of the time, but at least my body wasn't screaming for me to stand and run out of there. My mind drifted off focus from time to time, but I was able to pull it back.

During the next day, I had a major breakthrough. As I mentioned earlier, I am a compulsive overeater. During the afternoon sit, we had a food meditation. The leader passed around a bowl containing trail mix—banana chips, nuts, raisons, chocolate chips etc. We were told to pick out 4-5 items from the mix, but not to eat them. We were asked to think about how many people and places were involved in producing the items in our hands. Finally we were told to pick out one item. We were to hold it, feel its texture, smell it. Then we could put it in our mouth, but not bite into it. We were to notice if there was any taste, any physical reaction of the mouth to the food. Then we could bite into it. Did the taste flow out? What did we feel? Taste? Finally we were told to chew it as long as possible, savoring it as long as we could. We ate each item in our hand following the same process. Then we were told to use the same approach (As far as possible) when we went upstairs for dinner.

As a compulsive eater prone to wolfing food down, I found dinner eaten this was a sensuous experience. I tasted each bite of my potatoes, each spoonful of soup, each vegetable in my salad. I actually tasted what I ate. It took 45 minutes to finish a meal I would usually gulp down in ten minutes. I ate less than I usually do, but enjoyed it infinitely more. If I only take this one lesson home with me, and nothing else, the retreat will have been worth it. Of course it is easier to focus on the food when you are eating in silence.

That night began Holocaust Remembrance Day, and we lit a memorial candle. Now focusing on sits became infinitely easier for me. When I tired of focusing on my breath after 15-20 minutes, I could focus on the candle. I was still staying in the moment and not letting my mind run wild.

The instructors said that we would find after focused sits that we were more peaceful, clearer, more compassionate, more creative, and more able to solve formerly unsolvable problems. I had already found that true in solving my mind/body conflict. But now I found myself truly open to creativity. Stories, prayers, poems arose unbidden to my mind. I know I wasn't supposed to write, but remember impulse control has never been one of my virtues. I walked down past my rill to a river where the water cascaded over rocks. I sat there and wrote and wrote. Today, nearly two weeks after the retreat, I still find ideas pouring out of me.

On Wednesday, the third day of the retreat, I carried my pocketbook with me. Wednesday was usually my babysitting day, and I was in grandson withdrawal. My pocketbook had an outer panel that held pictures of my husband, my children, and my grandsons. Focusing on those pictures during a sit didn't feel like cheating. The pictures were right in front of me, so I was staying in the moment. Besides, one purpose of the retreat was to help us develop a sense of gratitude. Nothing makes me more aware of all I have to be thankful for than those pictures.

That afternoon sit was a revelation. About halfway through, I heard a giggle. I peeked open an eye, and I saw a young woman valiantly but unsuccessfully trying to suppress gales of laughter. The man next to her was also struggling mightily not to join the laughter. Soon titters erupted all over the room. None of us had been party to the original joke, but soon we were all engulfed in laughter. At the end of the sit, the instructors told us that such outbursts of laughter or crying were quite common during meditation retreats. Emotions bubble to the surface when we are vulnerable, and meditation increases vulnerability.

On the last day, just before lunch, we broke silence and talked about what the experience had been like for us, and what we had learned from it. Many people cried as they tried to give words to the inexpressible. Many besides myself had come with health issues, many far more serious than mine.

I mentioned that I wasn't usually a selfish person, but since my illness, I had gotten stuck in the "I." The experience of the meditation retreat had moved me back to the "we" of humanity. Now I could use my experience with illness to make me a better chaplain. Most of my geriatric congregants dealt with pain, illness, and depression with which I could now empathize.

On the way home, I couldn't stand the sound of the chatter of the radio. I had come to treasure the silence of the retreat.

Later I put on a tape of soft, classical music. On the way up, I had stopped at McDonald's for hamburger, fries and a soda. On the way home, I craved a salad!

If you ever have a chance to go to a meditation retreat, GO! It's good for the body, the mind, and the soul. I'm glad I hadn't known beforehand what the rules of the retreat would be, because I probably wouldn't have gone, and I would have missed a unique, invaluable experience.

"In the midst of winter I found there was within me an invincible summer."
(Camus)

Life Lessons I Learned From Cancer

1. Don't delay joy. Tomorrow is a gift, not a given.
2. Review your life. Make a list called "I'm glad I did" and one called "I wish I had." If the first list isn't much longer than the second one, change your priorities.
3. Prayer works! Ask friends of all faiths to pray for you . . . and pray for yourself and others!
4. Meditation heals the body as well as the spirit.
5. Pray for healing of body and healing of spirit. Even if you only get the latter, you will be able to live well for whatever time you have.

6. Your attitude helps or hinders the healing process.

7. Maintain an attitude of gratitude. Focus on your blessings not your burdens.

8. Psalm 118 says, "This is the day the Lord has made. Rejoice and be glad in it." Celebrate life every day.

9. Camus wrote "In the midst of winter, I found there is within me an invincible summer." Camus was right. We all contain within us the seeds of boundless optimism and incredible strength. We only need to learn how to make those blessings blossom.

10. If your spirit is whole, you are whole, no matter what parts are missing or non-functioning.

11. Never miss an opportunity to say "Thank you" or "I love you."

12. Mend relationships. Hold hands, not grudges.

13. Say "forgive me" and "I forgive you" whenever possible.

14. If tomorrow doesn't come, let the last words your loved ones heard from you be "I love you."

15. Keep pictures of things or people you love constantly in front of you so you never forget what you have to live for.

16. Plan for the future even when it isn't guaranteed.

17. Let people help you. It is a blessing to give. By being willing to receive, you allow someone else to fulfill the blessing of giving.

18. Don't let your pain or illness isolate you. Don't make yourself the focus of all your thoughts and conversations. Continue to care about others.

19. Surround yourself with those you love who love you.

20. Don't dwell on your pain in conversation unless you are speaking to someone who can actually do something about it.

21. Laugh often! Even illness can provide sources of laughter.

22. Trust your own instincts when it comes to your health and your body! No one-not even your doctor—knows you better than you do.

23. Never miss a chance to smell a rose, lick an icicle, hear the ocean, crunch through leaves, or hug a child.

Aging

Broken Vessels
(reprinted from **Manna For the Soul**)

> "Cast me not of in the time of old age;
> when my strength faileth, forsake me not." (Psalm 71:9)

The Bible says that God lovingly carved the letters of the Ten Commandments into the two tablets of stone. Then Moses came down the mountain, saw the Israelites with the golden calf, and threw the tablets down in anger, smashing them.

After the anger of God and Moses at the Israelites lessened, the story says Moses carved out two more stone tablets and carried them back up the mountain to be inscribed by God. When Moses brought this second set of tablets down, and placed them in the ark, legend says he also scooped up the broken pieces of the first tablets and placed them in the ark as well. The reason given for this is that a thing that is holy remains holy even after it is broken.

I contend that the same is true of people. People are holy because they contain the soul, the holy spark, and because they are created in the image of God. They remain holy even when they are broken, either physically or mentally, whether by genetics, birth, accident, injury, or age-related conditions. Someone who is not mentally or physically perfect is still holy. We honor God's holiness and our own when we continue to honor the holiness in all people regardless of their physical or mental condition.

It offends the holiness of a comatose person to be described or treated as "vegetables" in a "persistent vegetative state." It honors their holiness if we touch their hand or talk to them lovingly. Whether or not we believe they can hear us, God can hear us, and God is a loving parent who rejoices in seeing others treat all of God's children with love.

I often hear people say they can't visit hospitals or nursing homes. It frightens them; it depresses them; it reminds them of what they fear most in their own future. As someone who spends much of her time in hospitals and nursing homes, I really do understand those fears. But I also understand that the people in those places are also afraid and depressed, and those visits are what make their days bearable. And while I certainly wouldn't choose to end up in a facility, if I do, I hope the people I love will still visit me.

This reminds me of a story I once heard. An old man lived with his son, daughter-in-law and grandchildren. The family complained that the old man used up vital resources without contributing anything to the family. Finally the son decided that his father would have to die. The son built a wheelbarrow, put his father in it, and it wheeled it to the top of a mountain. As the son got to the top and was ready to push the wheelbarrow with his father in it over the cliff, his father said to him, "Throw me over if you must, but save the wheelbarrow. Your children will need it someday for you."

The truth is our children learn by what they see us do. If we show love, respect and compassion to our parents, that is what our children will learn. But if we show fear, anger, and resentment, that is what our children will learn.

Some people say, "I would visit but I don't know what to do or say. It depresses me to see him so confused." I've found when the other person has no words or the words make no sense, it is still possible to listen to the feelings beyond the words, the feelings conveyed by body language or facial expressions. By responding to those feelings, we can make contact "soul to soul."

A Game of Gin Rummy

I walked into the group home where Rita lived. I liked it. It was more like a home than an institution. Four other women lived there, all in various stages of Alzheimer's. I'd known Rita all my life, but although she was as sweet as always, it was clear that she didn't know who I was. When someone suggested a game of gin rummy, I was skeptical. Rita didn't remember old friends; she didn't remember what she had eaten an hour ago. How would she remember the rules to a card game? But we played—and she won all three games! And I realized two things. We had met on common ground and it was holy. And in those moments when she played and won, she was whole and she was happy.

Shabbat Shalom

Dr. Fishman came to services every week. He was in a geri-chair, in the end stages of Alzheimer's. I had never heard him speak. But still he came, accompanied by his lady friend Tonya. She was of a different faith, but she came with him every week to turn the pages of the prayer book, to pat his hand, to help him with juice served at the end of the service. I was touched by her dedication to him. Once when we were alone, Tonya talked about how bright Dr. Fishman had been, how interesting he had been to talk to, and how much she missed that communication.

At the end of the service, I went around shaking hands and greeting everyone. When I got to Dr. Fishman I said, "Shabbat Shalom." Tonya and I looked at each other in amazement as he clearly replied, "Shabbat Shalom," and then lapsed immediately back into silence.

I never heard him speak again, and only a few weeks later, he died, with Tonya by his side. But I often think of Dr. Fishman. I never question now whether what I do matters. Even if it was only once, only if it was only for a second, that prayer service got past a broken body, past a broken mind, and touched a living soul.

*Shabbat Shalom-Sabbath Peace, a traditional Jewish Sabbath greeting

The Power of Prayer

Since the experience with Dr. Fishman, I have had others like it. Prayer, especially when sung, has a way of reaching through the damaged outer body to find the intact soul. I know this. I have seen it. I have watched a woman who doesn't know where she is, possibly doesn't know who she is. But she hears the words to a prayer and she taps into some memory from her distant past. She begins to sing along with me. It gives me goosebumps. The moment is holy.

There are times when I sing at the start of Friday services in the nursing home, and the residents join in with me. It is a cacophony of sound that would make a music teacher cringe. But it touches my soul. It is the moment when Sabbath really arrives for me. And there are times when I am sure I can feel God's spirit in the room with us.

The Power of Music

Mr. Jones was in end-stage Alzheimer's. He didn't speak. He did seem to know his wife and smiled whenever she came. I was at a loss as to how to reach him when I visited.

Then in a visit to his wife, she mentioned that he used to love classical music. The next week I brought a concert tape and a small tape recorder with me. I sat next to his bed and played the music. His arm went up in the air, swaying in time to the music, as if he were conducting the orchestra. Once again, I was convinced that music, like prayer, can reach even those considered unreachable. I began taking music with me or chanting prayers out loud even when visiting comatose people. Does it reach them? I don't know. But it can't hurt! Holiness and spirituality mean encountering souls where they are. For this reason singing, playing music, even playing gin rummy can be holy I-thou encounters.

The Dimly Burning Wick

"The dimly burning wick shall he not quench." (Isaiah 42:3)

It was Friday afternoon. The Jewish residents in the nursing home filled the room for Shabbat services. I lit the Sabbath candles, two tapers of the same size, lit by the same match. Yet one candle's flame reached skyward, bright yellow-orange. The other produced a minute, barely visible flicker of blue. "That one isn't lit," called out several of the residents. I looked again and saw that the blue flicker was still barely visible. I said the blessings. As always I felt the spirit of Shabbat enter the room as the residents joined me in singing Shalom Aleichem, Peace To You.

But my eyes kept returning to those two candles, the one blazing; the other barely flickering. When it came time for the sermon, I threw out the prepared speech and talked about the candles instead.

It occurred to me that people were like those candles. Each of us contains a spark of godliness lit from the same Eternal Flame. Some of us let that light within shine forth to brighten the world and the people around us. Others keep the light so well hidden it is hard to believe a spark of godliness is anywhere within.

Then halfway through the service, the tiny spark finally blazed forth as high and bright as the other candle. The sight gave me hope for humanity. Even those who bury their spark in drugs, in cruelty, in vice, can change as the candle did. Even the worst offenders can sometimes learn to let the spark within them shine. I have known people like that little candle, people who wasted half a lifetime in crime, or in self-destructive behavior, people whose lives seemed wasted or worse, dangerous to themselves or others. And yet the spark was there within, waiting for them to let it shine. And the time came in their lives for reasons neither I nor they could explain, when they let the light shine forth and brighten the world they had previously darkened. The lesson is never give up on yourself. Never give up on anyone else. Never let others give up on themselves. The spark is there. The goal is to find the inspiration that will make it shine.

I think the metaphor of the candles is particularly appropriate for the nursing home residents. For some of them in pain, weak, frail, forgetful, life must seem like that flickering blue candle, but when they join with me in Sabbath prayer, for that moment their souls blaze forth brightly again.

I think of Dr. Fishman, the silent man in the final stages of Alzheimer's who at one service said "Shabbat Shalom." I realized that for that one brief moment, I had seen a flicker again become a flame. And that is why life, even when it is reduced to a flicker, is so precious. So I choose to work in nursing homes because I see beauty in "the dimly burning wick."

The Flickering Candle

Life is a flickering candle buffeted by the winds of time.

It glows briefly, flickers and goes out. But, oh, what that candle can do while yet it shines. It can brighten the darkest night, warm the coldest heart, or illuminate the path for those who have lost their way.

The challenge is not to bemoan the fact that you are only a candle, but to determine what kind of candle you want to be. Decide what you will do with that light while it still shines within you.

Will you be a birthday candle celebrating life?

. . . Or a yahrtzeit candle keeping those long gone alive in memory for future generations?

Will you be a Sabbath candle honoring God's holiness and fulfilling God's commandments?

Will you be a havdalah candle showing the world the difference between holy and profane?

Will you be the shamash candle bringing light to others?

Or a Hanukah candle keeping the light of freedom alive?

Will you be a Unity candle teaching the world to focus not on the external or superficial differences that separate us but on our common humanity that unites us?

Psalm 97:11 is often translated "Light is sown for the righteous." I prefer to interpret it "Light is sown by the righteous."

Will your life be a candle that sows light for others? Will it be the kind of light Hannah Senesh talked about when she said, "There are those whose radiance is visible on earth though they have long been extinct. There are people whose brilliance continues to light the world, though they are no longer living. These lights are particularly bright when the night is dark. They light the way for humanity." Hannah herself was one of those lights for humanity. Are you?

Yahrtzeit: The anniversary of the death of a loved one when a memorial candle is lit.

Shamash: The candle on the Hanukah menorah that is used to light the other eight candles.

Havdalah: The service that marks the end of the Sabbath and the beginning of the rest of the week.

Menorah: a special 7 or 9-branched candelabra.

Hanukah: a festival celebrating religious freedom by lighting a 9-branched menorah.

The Two Roses

I used to visit two women at a particular nursing home. Both were named Rose. Both were mentally sharp but wheelchair bound. Rose Love sat by the door, outside whenever weather permitted, and greeted all the staff, residents and guests who passed by. I lovingly called her "The Mayor of the Manor." She was the goodwill ambassador for the place. She greeted visitors by name, and asked about their families. She remarked about the helpful staff and the variety of activities in which she constantly remained involved. She was always busy knitting or reading between scheduled activities. She said she was grateful to have meals prepared for her so she no longer had to cook. She praised her wonderful children who took time to visit her every week.

Rose Crank sat outside of her room, waiting to waylay anyone who would listen to her gripe about the inattentive staff, the lack of worthwhile activities and the rotten food. She complained about her ungrateful kids who couldn't bother to visit more than once a week.

Both ladies had healthy minds and frail bodies. Both had the same activities, staff and food available. Both had weekly visits from their children. Both were telling the truth about the place as they saw it and experienced it. But their own attitudes and actions were largely responsible for their realities. It is true that the staff was often around Rose Love and avoided Rose Crank. But what the unhappy lady didn't realize was that by choosing to be a faultfinder rather than a joy finder, she created the isolated, unpleasant environment in which she lived. We can choose to be like Rose Love or Rose Crank. We are surrounded by both good and bad everyday. What we choose to focus on and how we choose to relate to others will color the kind of world we live in. It is our choice.

The Sermon

I began my talk to my congregation of elderly nursing home residents saying, "The rules for good living can be summed up in two Biblical phrases. 'You shall love the Lord your God with all your heart, with all your soul and with all your might.' And 'You shall love your neighbor as yourself.'

A shrill voice called out, "That's impossible. No one loves his neighbor as himself."

The original talk went out the window. A new one formed full-blown in its place.

I responded, "Improbable, yes! Rare, yes! Impossible, no! It might be impossible for you today. I have to admit it is impossible for me today. But I keep hoping."

Then I asked, "How many of you would risk your own life to save the life of your child?" Every hand went up. So I said, "See. It isn't impossible for any of us to love some people as ourselves."

The same insistent voice, "But that's not the same. That's family."

So I asked, "How many of you have a dear friend, not a relative, someone you love enough to risk your life to save theirs?"

Several hands went up. "So it isn't impossible to love some neighbors as yourself. It only seems impossible to love all neighbors as yourselves."

I had just returned from a meditation retreat the day before, and a story told there by Rabbi Sheila Peltz was emblazoned in my brain.

I told my congregants an adapted version of this true story.

"During World War II there was a stretcher bearer. His job was to go into the no man's land between two battling forces and bring back the wounded and the dead. He did the job faithfully, never taking a day off, even when he was entitled to it. His superiors noted his dedication and he was offered another safer job away from the front, but he asked to be allowed to remain as stretcher bearer. Regardless of age, regardless of race, regardless of religion, regardless even of which side the person had been fighting for, the stretcher bearer continued to pull the wounded to safety.

One day he returned weary and drenched in the blood of those he had tried to save. A fellow soldier approached him and asked, "How do you do it? You risk your own life every day. You come in covered with blood day after day. Don't you see the blood?"

The stretcher bearer replied quietly, "Yes, I see the blood. I see the earth bleeding. I see human beings bleeding. I see humanity bleeding. And *Leviticus 19* says, 'Do not stand idly by the blood of your neighbor.' That's why I do it."

I paused to wipe the tears from my eyes; then continued.

"Our Sabbath prayer book contains the prayer, 'May the day come when all humanity will recognize that it is one family.' Most of us can already love our family as ourselves. The secret of the stretcher bearer is that his soul had expanded enough to see the entire world as one family. Thus he could go out day after day and risk his life to save this human family. When the day comes that the rest of us can see the world as one family, we too will be capable of loving our neighbor as ourselves."

In Memoriam

The Eternal Light
(written in memory of Kyle Snyder)

Kyle managed to touch everyone who knew him in his short life. He was bright and courageous especially in facing his losing battle with cancer.

He was born on the fifteenth of the month and he died, two years and seven months later, on the fifteenth of the month.

After the funeral, his mother lit the shiva (memorial) candle, which true to its name, was expected to last seven days. As an only child, Kyle had been the light of his parents' lives. The light of the candle was somehow an extension of the light Kyle had brought into his parents' lives and they were no more ready to let it go out than they had been to see the light of his life extinguished.

The seventh day passed, and the candle continued to burn. The eighth day came and went and then the ninth and the tenth. On the thirteenth day, Kyle's aunt looked at the candle. She couldn't believe it. There didn't appear to be any wax left at all and yet the wick continued to burn.

The fourteenth day came and went and still the candle glowed. On the fifteenth day, Kyle's father came home from work and looked at the candle. It flickered one last time and went out. The miracle of the Hanukah lights that lasted for eights days was matched and surpassed by the miracle of Kyle's light.

Kyle and Dandelions
Photo by Bob Snyder, Kyle's Daddy

Yellow Flowers from Kyle by Sharon Snyder

Kyle used to pick me dandelions all the time. He would say, "Here, mama, a yellow flower for you." I loved the very first one he picked for me, the very last one he picked for me, and every one in between. I cherished those beautiful yellow flowers as much as I cherished my beautiful little boy.

After Kyle passed away, we decided to plant a yellow rose bush outside of our home, the house Kyle lived in his entire young life. We didn't know what to expect with this rose bush, as we had never planted one before. When we planted it in late spring of that year, it was full of beautiful yellow blooms. After the last flower died, a flower expert told me not to expect any more flowers until the next year. To my surprise though, the next bloom we got happened to be on my birthday, July 21st. I felt as though it was a special birthday present my little angel had given his mama for my birthday. It continued to bloom throughout the summer, giving both my husband and myself a little peace in what was left of our broken hearts.

Kyle's Rosebush
Photo by Bob Snyder

The next time the rose bush bloomed happened to be the following spring . . . on Mother's Day. Yes, once again my little angel had given his mama a yellow flower. Then what began to happen was I would receive these oh so special roses every birthday and Mother's Day like clockwork. The most fascinating thing of all was that every birthday, the number of roses on this day would be the number of how old Kyle would be that year. The last year we spent at our house that we shared together, there were 7 roses that bloomed on my birthday.

It was very difficult to leave that house. We put it up for sale and left the end of summer last year. We had thought to take the rose bush with us and transplant it in our new home, but decided against that in fear it would not transplant well. On occasion, we will drive by our beloved home we shared with our precious Kyle. This past Mother's Day, we took a drive past the house. We noticed that not even one rose was in bloom, not even close. This had been the first year that our Kyle's rose bush did not bloom on Mother's Day. I thought it would break my heart not to receive my special yellow flowers from my little guy, but it actually warmed my heart, because at that moment I realized that our oldest son had moved with his family to our new home, to live together forever connected.

Yellow Ladybugs and Other Beautiful Gifts
by Sharon Snyder

After Kyle was diagnosed with leukemia, he took a liking to ladybugs. I'm not sure when it happened exactly, but as time went by, he would point them out more and more. He began to get many ladybug gifts from us and everyone who wanted to put a smile on his beautiful face.

Kyle passed away on October 15th, 1998. Several days later we had his service. When we came back home after everything ended, I wound up in Kyle's bedroom with my two nieces and Kyle's cousins, Jessica and Christin. I think we wound up there because that is where we felt closest to him. I showed them a poster that Kyle's Aunt Shelley had made for him when he was in the hospital. It was a collage of Kyle's favorite things. We looked at all of the pictures and I began to ask them different questions such as, "What do you see here that Kyle loved?" They both pointed out several pictures of things like broccoli and French fries. They had both mentioned that there were things on there that he didn't especially like and many things that weren't included. So that is when I asked, "Okay, what is missing that Kyle loved?" One of my nieces said, "Aunt Sharon, Kyle loved ladybugs." I said, "Yes, he did love ladybugs." Well at that moment the room got very warm. It is important to note that Kyle's room was always cool because of where it was situated. It seemed as though it became overly warm right when we were talking about Kyle's love for ladybugs. So I went to the window to draw the blinds. When I raised them and then opened the window, there flew onto the screen one ladybug and then two more. I said, "Look girls! There are three ladybugs on the screen." They both looked at these beautiful ladybugs with me. After what seemed like a long time, one flew away and then another, and shortly after the other one followed.

After our wonderful encounter with Kyle's ladybugs, we began to see more and more of them. My husband would have one fly to him every time he would do some work around the house or at his workplace. Kyle loved to follow his daddy around the house and pretend to work right along side of him. He even went to his workplace with his daddy and was his little helper. Even now, after we moved, nearly six years later, my husband Bob will still get his little helper flying in whenever he has a project he is working on at home.

These ladybugs always came to us whenever we felt as though we couldn't take one more moment of grief. I should mention that Kyle's favorite color was yellow. I never knew that yellow ladybugs existed, that is until after my sweet Kyle passed away. One day after we planted Kyle's yellow rose bush, a yellow ladybug appeared on it! After the first experience we later encountered several more yellow ladybugs. I remember seeing our ladybugs right into January the year that Kyle died. I couldn't believe that they could still be around that time of the year. What amazed me most was, I only remember seeing ladybugs every once in a while, and the year that Kyle passed away, I saw more of them than I probably did my entire life put together.

Approximately six months after Kyle died, I was going through the newspaper when I stumbled across a little article about ladybugs. I was never big on reading the newspaper, especially during the week, and this was the first time I had ever seen this particular section. It was a children's question and answer segment. I almost skimmed right over it when I saw a picture of a ladybug. It caught my attention, but what follows is what was most inspiring. This article said that ladybugs were named after Mary, and that people thought there was something heavenly about ladybugs, and that they were a gift from G-d. I thought it was especially amazing when I saw that the two girls who had written in to ask why ladybugs were called ladybugs, had the same names as Kyle's two cousins.

During the early part of our grief, an old acquaintance of mine had found out about Kyle. She took the time to mail me a handwritten card saying how sad she was for us and to please call if I needed someone to talk to. On the card itself was a picture of a ladybug hugging a pillow. Once again, there was that cute little bug sending some comfort. It turns out, this acquaintance turned into one of the most important people in my life.

I have met many other bereaved parents during my travels, and to my amazement, many of their children had loved ladybugs as well. Ladybugs have become synonymous to Kyle with everyone who either knew him while he was here with us or who has had the opportunity to meet him through us after his passing. I strongly feel that Kyle sends us his ladybug friends from time to time to let us know that he will always be a part of us forever.

* For information about an organization begun in Kyle's memory to help children with cancer and their families, please visit www.kissesforkyle.org.

The Butterfly (Written in memory of Jackie)
Think of her but do not cry,
lovely fragile, like a butterfly.
She touched down then quickly left,
At first we wept, our hearts bereft.
But remember now and do not cry,
Her spirit soared like a butterfly.
She graced our lives for a brief minute;
Our world was sweeter while she was in it.

My Friend is Dead (Written in memory of Joan)
My friend is dead, and I never said goodbye.
She died too soon and much too far away.
If only I had called more often.
If only I had seen her just once more,
but I didn't, and now it's too late.
My friend is dead, and I never said goodbye.

A Light Has Been Extinguished (In memory of Mark)
Not quite a man;
no longer a boy.
Just on the brink
of life, of love, of learning.
Handsome, focused, bright,
a world of possibilities
shone before him.

How could it be?
Why should it be
that such a light
has been extinguished?

A Youth Facing Mortality

He should go to college.
He should go on dates.
He should go on vacation.
He should not go in the ground!
He is too young to die.
I am too young for all these tears.
Then an awful thought arises.
Then appears an awesome fear.
If he can die, can I?

Go Gently Into that Good Night

(with apologies to Dylan Thomas)
Go gently, beloved, into that goodnight.
Old age may go in peace at close of day.
Rest, rest, in God's Eternal Light.

I'm Not Afraid

I'm not afraid my life will end
for death comes gently, as a friend.
I'll slip softly into life's ebb and flow
for into God's loving hands I go.
Do not fear that I'll be alone;
God is with me; I am God's own.
As I leave, all pain will cease.
And I'll enter into God's world of peace.
I will not fret for you, my love.
You'll find comfort from above.
Nor will I fear when we're apart;
I will live on in your loving heart.
And when your earthly bonds set you free,
You'll come to rejoin our God . . . and me.

A Prayer from One Living With Alzheimer's

The disease takes away my memories.
It may take away my control.
But don't let it touch my spirit.
Don't let it touch my soul.
It may take away my language,
and play tricks upon my mind.
But through it all, despite it all,
keep me gentle, sweet and kind.

After a Death from Alzheimer's

We are not here to mourn a death, but to celebrate a life.
Over the past few years we saw our friend die by inches.
Those who love her have already mourned each little loss,
each little death, each lost ability, each forgotten memory.
Now she is free of that terrible illness
that took her away from herself,
and away from those who loved her, one piece at a time.
In the past years, Alzheimer's took away many of her memories-
Fortunately, it could not take away our memories of her.
It took away her strength and independence,
but not the lessons of strength and independence
she had taught by her example.
It took away her desire to do the things she once loved to do,
but not our memories of the loving things she did for us.
It took away her ability to care for others,
but not the legacy of caring that we learned by knowing her.
Alzheimer's victory was shallow and temporary.
Once more she is in a place
where she can watch over those she loves.
And once more we are in a place
where we can remember her as she was,
vibrant, strong, loving and caring.
We do not mourn a death today;
we celebrate a life well-lived.

Thoughts in Sadness

A teary raindrop knocking at my window,
does it, too, want refuge from this dreary day?
No, you can't come in here
too many rainy teardrops crowd this room.
There is no room for you.
Your rainy water is not sad-
the rainbow always follows.
In here there is just rain-I cry
Stay out dear teardrop—
there will be a sun for you,
but mine is dead.

The Eulogy

"I'm sad today. He was a nice man. He was kind to everyone," Ilene, a lovely, sweet lady in the middle stages of dementia, said to me as I approached her. Danny, the eighty-nine year old man she spoke of had been a long-time resident of an assisted living facility. He was kind of the elder statesman of the place. He often sat on the front porch of the place, greeting all visitors and staff, as he waited for his lady friend to pick him up.

As the chaplain of the facility, I had come on this day to lead a memorial service for Danny. While I waited for the residents to gather, I heard Ilene several times repeating, "I'm sad today. He was a nice man. He was kind to everyone."

During the service, I spoke of his intelligence, his kindness, his business acumen. Finally I asked if any of the residents who knew him wanted to speak. Several residents spoke warmly about him, and then Ilene piped up. "I'm sad today. He was a nice man. He was kind to everyone."

The service continued, punctuated periodically by, "I'm sad today. He was a nice man. He was kind to everyone." Others looked at her annoyed, and tried to hush her up, but I was touched by her moving eulogy, repeated almost like a mantra.

And I really believe when Danny goes before the throne of judgment, the words God will weigh most heavily in his favor are the words from a broken life he touched, "I'm sad today. He was a nice man. He was kind to everyone."

My Husband Was Here Last Night

Bella and her husband Vince had been inseparable for nearly 50 years. So great was his love for her that at age 90, Vince had and survived quadruple bypass surgery, so he could continue to care for her. But even that love couldn't keep him going forever. I visited Bella days after her beloved Vince died. She said, "My husband was here last night." For a moment, I wondered if she had suppressed the memory of his death. But then she added, "He came back to make sure I was all right. I wanted to go with him, but he told me it wasn't my time yet. But he promised he'd be back for me soon." Was she dreaming? Was she hallucinating? Maybe, but I'm not sure. I do know a few weeks later on the night Bella died, her niece stayed in the room with her all night. The next day, I spoke to the niece who said, "I must have been dreaming, but I really thought I was awake last night, when just for a second I thought I saw Uncle Vince in the room. I got up and checked on Bella, and she had just died." Was the niece dreaming, too, or are there loves so strong that they can outlast even death. I prefer to believe that Vince really came for Bella as he had promised.

Tell Nina It's a Girl

Sometimes people who are close to death seem to have a foot in both worlds. Nina was eight months pregnant with her first child when her beloved grandmother was dying. Nina hadn't found out the sex of her baby. Nina visited her grandmother often. But on one particular night, Nina was exhausted and had to go home. Nina's mother stayed at her mother's bedside. The grandmother whispered, "Tell Nina it's a girl," and then lapsed into final silence. Did the grandmother know or did she guess? Nina's girl, named for her grandmother, was born a few weeks later.

Not Yet

Pauline was dying. All medical indications were that death was imminent. She had lapsed into a coma and no longer responded to the family. The family called me in to pray with them. As I said Viddui, the Jewish Final Confession, for Pauline, her eyes opened wide and she turned to look at me, as if to say "Not yet." One of her children said, "I know what she's waiting for. Her anniversary is next week. She's waiting until then to join my father." How does a dying woman hang on beyond all medically explainable time? How does she even know the date in a comatose state? I don't know, but I do not believe that it is a coincidence that Pauline died just moments after her anniversary date arrived.

Manna For the Soul

I am Peace

I love the saying "I am peace."(Psalm 120:7). What an incredible gift I have. I have the ability to give myself peace of mind. I have the opportunity to make every encounter peaceful rather than confrontational. And when I choose peace as my way of life, I choose to live Torah because "its ways are ways of pleasantness and all its paths are peace."

People often ask me why I wasn't angry or resentful when my first husband left me and married another woman. The answer is, for a while, I was. But then I realized that the anger was hurting me and preventing me from moving on with my life. I had the ability to give myself peace by forgiving them. In hindsight, I can see that I made the right decision. I don't know what I would have gained by holding onto the hurt and anger, but I know what I gained by letting go of it. My ex-husband and I are friends now. That makes life infinitely easier for our children. By letting go of the anger at him in specific and at men in general, I was eventually able to find the right relationship for me.

I can't say that all things that happen are good, but I can say that even from the worst things, some good can result. If I can look at people who have hurt me with pity or sorrow rather than anger, I can forgive them, be at peace with them, and be at peace with myself.

I am not always at peace, as anyone who has seen me behind the wheel at rush hour or standing in a long line can attest. But I'm working on it! I know that road rage or impatience in line hurts me. It raises my blood pressure and it ruins my mood. And where am I going that is so important that it is worth ruining my health and my peace of mind and someone else's day to get there five minutes sooner?
Peace starts with a state of mind. And my state of mind influences the moods of other people with whom I have contact. If I blast my horn or shout at a cashier, I lose my inner peace and the people affected by my actions lose theirs. This in turn affects the way they relate to other people that day. My snarl or smile has a rippling affect throughout the day in ways I can't even comprehend.
When I choose peace as my way of life, I am involved in repairing the

world. So I am striving to live my life in such a way that I can honestly say, "I am peace."

The Death of a Wicked Man
(Reprinted from **Manna For the Soul**)

Morris Lev knew that he was a wicked man. He knew it because his father Jacob had been telling him so since the day of Morris's birth, the day his mother died giving birth to him. What could be more wicked than killing his own mother?

As he grew older, he tried to hide his wickedness by doing good deeds for others. He worked hard to support his father who drank to forget the pain of losing his wife. Jacob took the money Morris earned. After all, Morris owed him that and much more than he could ever pay. But Jacob made it clear that the money would never purchase forgiveness. Jacob made clear every day of the sixteen years that Morris lived with him that Morris was too wicked to ever be forgiven. In his drunken rages Jacob made it clear with words, with his fists, and with his walking stick, that Morris was not and never would be forgiven for his sins.

Finally Jacob died. Morris began to aid the poor, feed the hungry, and do chores for his ailing neighbors. He hoped that others would not know how wicked he was if he spent his life doing good deeds.

But then Mordechai and Eva Gardner moved next door. Eva with her full-bosomed beauty and her unaffected good nature caught Morris's attention, and he wanted her. "Thou shalt not covet thy neighbor's wife, another commandment I've broken," thought Morris. One night he found himself in a passionate embrace with Eva when he awoke with a start to find his underwear shamefully damp. He had committed adultery, if only in his dreams, and he had spilled his seed, two more commandments he had broken. He was terrified that his evil would be discovered so he took great care never to be alone with Eva. He even helped Mordechai with a loan when his neighbor's business failed so no one would guess how wicked Morris was.

Finally it came time for Morris to die and he was terrified. He had fooled people into thinking he was a kind, generous man, but God would know the truth. At last he was led with trembling and trepidation before the Throne of Judgment.

The booming Voice said to him, "Morris Lev, you believe you are a wicked man, don't you? "Yes," whispered Morris. "And you believe you are a murderer?" Hanging his head in shame, Morris mumbled, "Yes."

"You are not!" the Voice thundered. "Your father was drunk the day you were born. He stumbled into your mother and knocked her down. He was responsible for her premature labor and her death, and he nearly killed you as well. He blamed you because he couldn't face his own guilt."

"You believe you are an adulterer but you are not. You had a dream. You are not responsible for your dreams."

"But," Morris sighed, "I coveted my neighbor's wife." "Yes, you did. But you didn't act on your desire. In the end, it is not what you think or feel that matters; it is what you do that counts. When King David coveted Bathsheba, he sent her husband to the battlefront to die and then he took her. When you coveted Eva, you made certain you were never alone with her. You saved her husband from financial ruin. You were more righteous than King David! You are a righteous man, Morris Lev. You are a good man. The righteous man is not the one without evil inclinations. The truly righteous man is the one who, when faced with temptations, does not give into them. As it says in **Mishnah Avot** 4:1, "Who is strong?: The one who masters his evil impulses."

Finally Morris Lev knew that he was a good man. He knew it because his Father told him so on the day Morris died.

There is Always Hope
(In Memory of Marlyn Chakov Fein)

> Hope is the thing with feathers
> That perches in the soul
> And sings the tune without the words
> And never stops-at all. (Emily Dickinson)

Monica Dawson read the Emily Dickinson poem out loud, patted her protruding stomach, and said, "Hope!" That's what I want to name her. I just know it's a girl."

Jerry Dawson just looked at his wife sadly. "Why is it so important to you to have this baby? This pregnancy is killing you. You're doing this for me, aren't you? So I'll have something to live for. So I won't be so alone after . . ." His voice trailed off.

"After I'm gone," Monica continued. "Yes, I'm partly doing it for you and my parents, so you'll still have a part of me. But most of all I'm doing it for myself. This pregnancy isn't killing me; the cancer is killing me. I may not be able to beat Death, but if I can trade my life for a life, I'll feel that I at least cheated Death. This is a miracle pregnancy. The doctors never thought it possible. Imagine that we didn't even know that I am pregnant and I'm in my sixth month. The doctors thought the nausea was from the medication and the bloated stomach was another tumor. And then we worried that the cancer and the medication might have harmed the baby, but all the pre-natal tests show that the baby is fine. This is our miracle baby. This baby wants to be born. And when she is born, I won't ever really be gone. A part of me, of us, will still be here." Jerry's eyes filled with tears as he walked over and hugged his wife.

A mere month after that conversation, Jerry was in the delivery room. He squeezed Monica's frail hand as he watched her struggle though another contraction.

"Breathe, honey, breathe," he coaxed gently, and then he kissed her hand lightly when he saw that the spasm had passed.

He was grateful to be in the delivery room. He realized that under normal circumstances the doctors wouldn't have allowed a husband to be present at such a high-risk delivery. But these weren't normal circumstances and this was not an ordinary baby. Monica tensed up again and pushed one last time, and the tiny head emerged. One more push and she was out.

The doctor held the motionless infant momentarily and then he whirled into action. He ripped off his facemask and frantically breathed life into the tiny child. She was barely bigger than the palm of his hand. Afterwards, he realized that his gesture had been foolish, unsanitary and unnecessary in a room equipped with the latest neo-natal devices-but at the moment he had lost his professional objectivity. "Damn it," he thought. "This baby has fought so hard to be born. Her mother has struggled so hard to give her life." He wanted this baby to live.

At last a little squeal. Not the lusty cry he would have liked to hear, but a pathetic peep told him the child was alive. "Get her to neo-natal intensive care. Stat!" he barked.

Monica opened her eyes. "Did you say *her?* I knew it was a girl!"

The doctor looked at the anxious couple gravely. "You have a daughter, but after all you've been through I don't want to lie to you. I can't give you false hope. She is a seven month preemie I doubt that she weighs more than three pounds. And with all of the other complications of the pregnancy-well I just don't know. The odds aren't much better than fifty-fifty, so don't raise your hopes."

Monica replied, "But we are going to raise our Hope, doctor. That's what we've named her, Hope. She's going to make it. Fifty-fifty isn't such bad odds. She beat worse odds than that just to get here. She's a fighter just like me. I fought to give her life; she'll fight to keep it."

Six weeks later the doctor and Jerry Dawson stood by Monica's bed. "Well, I never thought I'd see this day," the doctor said. "Hope weighs five pounds now. She can go home tomorrow. She really is a miracle baby."

Jerry looked at his wife lying motionless on the bed. "And Monica, when can I take her home?"

The doctor's eyes clouded. "I'm afraid there is only one miracle per family. I'm sorry, Jerry. Monica won't be going home. It's only a matter of time now. There's no hope."

Monica struggled to open her eyes and look one more time at the baby picture that was always clenched in her hand. Just before she closed her eyes for the last time, she murmured, "Yes, there is Hope. There is always Hope."

*For more information about the Marlyn Fein Chapter of the Fox Chase Cancer Center see www.fccc.edu/

Kaddish in a Closet

It was July 1976, three months after my father's death. At home I had settled into a comfortable ritual of attending Friday night services to say Kaddish. I was accompanied by my children, twins Rob and Jodie, nearly five, and two-year-old Stacy. For that year, and that year only I never had to force them to accompany me. Maybe it was their way to honor the memory of their Poppy. Or maybe they knew that I needed them with me, but they may never know the depth of the comfort their presence afforded me. I remember the first Shabbat after my father's death, when I stood shaking in raw pain, and with a quavering voice, I recited the words of the Mourner's Kaddish. I really believe my trembling legs would have collapsed beneath me had I not drawn strength and comfort from Stacy who had fallen asleep in my arms. As the year progressed, it became a standing joke with the rabbi. During his sermon he would glance over at Stacy. When she nodded off, he said he knew it was time to end his talk.

Anyway, July 1976, we were on a family vacation at the seashore. From my earliest childhood, when I hunted for shells on the beach with my grandfather, the shore had been my place for peace, for joy, for renewal of the soul. I really needed the solace of the place that year.

It was the same shore where, as a ten-year-old, I had first felt God's presence. I'd been sitting on a rock listening to the crash of the waves, watching the endless, rhythmic roll of the water, refreshed by the cool, salty spray that splashed up on me. Suddenly I felt this sense of peace envelop me. In my child's mind, I thought I'd felt God's hug.

But this July morning when I went to pray, I would not feel God's hug. The only synagogue I could find nearby was an Orthodox shul. I decided to go to the Friday morning service to say Kaddish. The children were still sleeping so I left them with their father and I went to services alone, the only time the entire year that I did so. I timidly entered the shul in time for the 8:30 a.m. service. The small group of men seemed startled to see me. "What are you doing here?" one asked. When I said I had come to pray, they explained that women never came to the morning service and the women's section upstairs was closed off. When I insisted that I had to say Kaddish, they were in a quandary. It was an Orthodox shul. A woman could not pray with the men, but they wouldn't turn away anyone, even a woman, who wanted to say Kaddish. Finally they handed me a prayer book and led me into a book closet in the back of the sanctuary. I don't ever remember feeling so alone in my life. No warm supportive congregation. No rabbi smiling at me as my toddler fell asleep in my lap. No warm little arms linked through mine on either side of me. I didn't feel prayerful there. I couldn't feel God's presence. I followed the service in my little cell until the first reading of the Kaddish. It wasn't really the Mourner's Kaddish which comes at the end of the service, but I couldn't stand the isolation of the place a moment longer. My intentions were good. I said the prayer, closed my book, and tiptoed out.

Later in the day, barefoot, ankle-deep in the ocean I loved, surrounded by my laughing, loving children, I said the Kaddish again. This one might not have had the hechsher of rabbinic authority, but I think it met with God's and my father's approval.

Mourner's Kaddish—a prayer of praise to God read by family members of one who died. It is believed that the greatest honor one can do for someone who has died is to continue to praise God in memory of the deceased.

Shul-synagogue

Hechsher-official stamp of rabbinic approval

Isn't She Beautiful

Bella sat bent over in her wheelchair, her body twisted from the ravages of arthritis and Parkinson's and a stroke. People walked past her in the hall, ignoring her. She was just one more old broken body in a nursing home full of them.

Finally a nurse saw her there and wheeled her into the room of her husband of 50 years. He smiled as she came into the room and he said to the nurse, "Isn't she beautiful?" Bella's face lit up at the sound of his voice, and I realized it was true. She was beautiful.

Daddy Help Me! (In Memory of Arthur Kasser)

I knelt in the soggy grass, which was drenched from a solid week's worth of rain. I brushed my fingers past my lips and gently touched them to the white marker that said:

> **Alan Kimball May 6 1916-April 19 1975**
> **Beloved father and grandfather**

My mind traveled back twenty-two years to envision the dark-haired three-year-old with serious brown eyes who was balancing on the edge of the pool at the swim club until she tripped, and toppled into the deep water. "Daddy, help me!" I remembered awaking in the arms of my father who stood soaking wet in his new sports coat and slacks. He never dressed for the swim club. In fact, he hated the sun. He only went to the swim club because I loved it.

My thoughts drifted to my teenage years when no boy had been good enough for his little girl. I remembered the night I had introduced dad to Ron, my fiancé. I really think dad was jealous of Ron then, but in time they became good friends.

And finally I remembered that day, Saturday April 19th. Ron was out playing baseball that afternoon. My infant twins were upstairs napping in their cribs; I was reading, and dad was spending Saturday in his favorite way. He was at my house, half-dozing on the old black recliner with one baseball game on television and another blaring on the radio.

Suddenly I smelled smoke and dashed upstairs. The hall was already filled with thick black smoke as I raced into the twins' bedroom and grabbed a child under each arm. The fire was spreading quickly, the smoke burned my eyes, and the children squirmed in fright in my arms. "Daddy, help me!" I shouted.

Oblivious to the smoke, he rushed up the steps and into the nursery. He realized that we couldn't get back down the stairway so he told me to lower myself out the window. Thank God we had bought the split-level instead of the two-story house, I remember thinking, as I made the drop. He handed the children down to me. I screamed for him to jump, but he didn't.

For days I blamed myself. Why did I call him for help? Why didn't he jump? Finally Ron told me the truth. "Stop blaming yourself. You know your father would have gladly died for you and the kids, but that day, he also died for himself. He had just found out a few days before that he had terminal cancer. He was trying to work up the nerve to tell you that day. He hated the thought of what a slow, painful death would do to him—and to you. At least this way, by saving you and the kids, his death was meaningful and quick."

I kissed my hand to the stone again, and rose. As I turned, a man stepped out of the shadows and grabbed my arm. I saw the leer on his face and the knife in his hand. I took an involuntary step backward, but he tightened his grip on my arm. I offered him what little money I had, but he said he'd get to that later. First he wanted to have some fun. As he stepped closer to me, I panicked. "Daddy, help me!"

I felt the ground tremble, and I fell backward. When I awoke, a medic and a policeman stood over me. "You were very lucky, young lady," he said. This man is the rapist-murderer we've been chasing for six months." I looked up and saw the man lying in a hole where my father's grave should have been. His leg was twisted under him and the strange position of his head immediately told me he was dead. "All of this rain must have washed away the foundation under this new grave," the policeman commented. "Lucky for you, it collapsed when he stepped on it."

Well, the policeman is entitled to his explanation of what happened there, and I am entitled to mine. And I no longer felt sad and alone because I realized that even in death, daddy was there to help me when I needed him.

The Twins

My twins were no more alike than other brothers and sisters. Sean was tall and broad with a round face, straight blond hair, and twinkling blue eyes. Shannon was dainty and petite, with brownish-blond ringlets and a tiny face with huge, serious brown eyes, like a doll in a Keane print. They played, they fought, and they ignored each other like most siblings.

In the midst of their daily squabbles, it was easy to forget what a strong bond there was between them. Sean was usually out front playing with his friend Mikey; Shannon was generally next door with her friend Lisa. The twins rarely spent much time together. But there was an inexplicable bond between them that was only strengthened by distance.

For example, I remember the incident that happened when they were three years old. We were all supposed to go to Philadelphia to visit my in-laws. But at the last minute, Shannon awoke with a fever, so we decided that my husband Roger would go into Philadelphia with Sean, and I would stay home with Shannon.

Roger and Sean left on Saturday. By Sunday, Shannon's mysterious fever had disappeared, so I let her play outside in the yard. About 2:00, she suddenly started screaming. She limped over to me crying, "My foot hurts, Mommy." She held up her left foot for my inspection, but I could find nothing wrong with it. I held her in my lap and tried to soothe her, but it seemed as if she didn't hear me. About 2:30, I began to think that maybe I should take her to the doctor's office. And yet, there didn't seem to be anything wrong with her foot. I massaged it, thinking maybe she had a charley horse in the arch of her foot. But nothing helped her. Then as suddenly as it had started, the crying stopped, and she hopped off my lap and ran back to the swings to play. I was dumbfounded. She hadn't been faking. The look of pain on her face had been too real. I was still musing about her strange behavior when the phone rang. It was Roger. His first words were, "Don't worry he's fine, but..." I interrupted and finished his sentence, "Sean hurt his foot about an hour ago but now he's fine." I don't know how I knew it, but I did. I realized that Shannon's pain had been a real empathy with her brother's pain even though he was two hundred miles away. Sean had stepped on some broken glass and needed five stitches to close the cut. When I told Roger about Shannon's behavior, he was mystified. But such an unusual event didn't happen again, until last week, three days after their fifth birthday.

It was Tuesday evening when Shannon went tearing into the street on her new Hot Wheels. The driver of the car never saw her coming. The poor guy was distraught, but it really wasn't his fault. I hated him momentarily, but I soon realized that he was suffering almost as much as I was.

Tuesday night and Wednesday passed like an eternity for us. Shannon was in a coma. The doctors knew that she had internal injuries, but she was too weak even for exploratory surgery to determine the extent of the damage. It's funny. When I went to see her, so tiny and fragile and pale in that hospital bed with the tubes and the monitors attached everywhere, my first reaction was, "Thank God that beautiful face wasn't even scratched." I must have been in shock. I guess we all were. Finally the doctor gave me a sedative and sent me home. He promised to call me the minute there was any change. I hated to leave, but Shannon didn't even know I was there, and Sean needed me.

The change in that kid was amazing. Usually finding Sean is like chasing the wind. He's usually in and out, up and down the steps a million times a day. But that Wednesday, he was just a walking shadow. He ate nothing, said nothing. He would just sit in a corner staring into space, get up, wander aimlessly, and sit down again. It was frightening. I tried to talk to him, reassure him, but I couldn't reach him.

That Wednesday night, well actually it was Thursday morning about 4:00 a.m., Sean came shrieking into our bedroom. Roger and I jumped up-we hadn't been able to sleep anyway. Sean was ashen with pain, clutching his stomach. I grabbed him, rocking him gently, trying to soothe him. But it was if he wasn't there. He didn't hear me, but I heard him and what he said jolted me out of bed so quickly, Sean tumbled off my lap onto the bed.

I ran to the phone and called the pediatric intensive care. "Nurse Peterson, please check Shannon. I know there is something wrong with her stomach. I'll wait on the phone."

She came back and reported that Shannon was still in a coma. "Look, please check her blood pressure. Please see if her stomach is swollen. Maybe it's internal bleeding. I know something is wrong." She started to say something, but I was so hysterical, she decided to check again. I waited on the phone for what seemed like hours-probably about ten minutes, until a different nurse picked up the phone. "You'd better come right away. There is internal bleeding and Shannon is being prepared for immediate emergency surgery. Dr. Corbett is on his way."

Roger was already dressed and holding the still-sobbing Sean. We raced to the hospital. Roger went into the waiting room where the families of surgical patients wait. I took Sean to the emergency room. The doctors could find nothing wrong with him, but they gave him a shot to calm him, and admitted him for observation. I asked for and obtained permission for him to get a bed in Shannon's room. About 6:30, his pain stopped and he fell asleep in my arms. I put him in bed, stroking his hair, and wondered: Had I heard him right when he came crying into my bedroom? Had he really said, "Shannon's tummy hurts' or had my exhausted brain scrambled the message? In any case, if she lived, he had saved her.

I joined Roger in the waiting room. The doctor finally called about 7:00. Shannon was extremely weak and she had lost a lot of blood, but she had survived the surgery. She was still in a coma, but the internal bleeding had been stopped. It was still touch and go with her, we knew that, but at least the bleeding had stopped.

I fell into an uneasy sleep in the waiting room. When I went into Shannon's room at 11:00 Thursday morning, Sean's bed was empty. There he was asleep in the chair next to Shannon's bed, holding her hand. I called the nurse into the room and she explained, "When I looked into the room two hours ago, I found him there, like a little old man, holding her hand and talking to her. I'd never seen anything like it. He wouldn't leave her side, even to eat. I tried to pick him up and put him back into his bed, but Shannon stopped me. She was in a semi-conscious state, and she tightened her grip on his hand. I asked Dr. Corbett, and he thought it might be best for both of them if Sean stayed by her side. Sean only left her once, to go to the bathroom, and Shannon was very restless when he was gone. But as soon he as returned, she mumbled, 'Sean stay here' and drifted back into a deep sleep.

He was amazing. He never left her side the whole time I was there. He kept talking to her although she kept drifting in and out of consciousness. He even slept in the small chair beside her. All day Thursday and Friday he stayed with her, barely eating or sleeping. I was worried about his health, but the doctor said the boy was fine-that Sean should have been released from the hospital except that his presence was obviously doing Shannon so much good.

On Friday evening, I went down to the cafeteria. When I came up, the chair by Shannon's bed was empty. Sean was racing up and down the room, flying the toy plane that he hadn't touched for nearly a week. He looked at me and said, "I all better now. I wanna go home and play with Mikey."

I looked over at Shannon and there were those big, solemn eyes staring at me as she managed the faintest hint of a smile.

Entrances to Holiness
(reprinted from **Manna For the Soul**)

"Entrances to holiness are everywhere."
(Lawrence Kushner, **Honey From the Rock**, p.48)

When we go through trying times and feel that God isn't there for us, it isn't because God isn't open to us; it is because we aren't open to God. We are like Jacob who slept through a holy encounter. The next morning when he awoke, he realized, "God was in this place and I didn't know it." (*Genesis* 28:16) Entrances to holiness are everywhere, but sometimes we are so busy that we walk right past them, or like Jacob, sleep right through them.

There is holiness when we stop to appreciate the beauty and wonder of the world around us. After an ice storm, I am usually so busy shivering, scraping ice off the car, stepping tentatively with eyes focused on the slippery surface, that I forget to look up at the shining crystal boughs arching over my head. But on those rare occasions when I remember to look up at the magnificent pristine landscape, I am in awe of God's creation.

When my twins were born, I was usually too exhausted from sleep deprivation and too busy changing diapers to think about the millions of cells and atoms that had to come together in just the right pattern to create those two lives. But now that I have time to think about it, I realize that I gave birth to two miracles.

There is holiness in I-thou encounters with God. I have always found it easier to find entrances to holiness in places of great physical beauty, such as Banff, Niagara Falls, the Grand Canyon and the ocean.

I remember one time when I was quite young, I was sitting on some rocks by the ocean as the tide came in. I was mesmerized by the constant roll of the breakers, by the crash as the waves broke on the rocks, by the salt spray that showered down on me. And as I sat there, I felt this sense of calm, of peace, of contentment settle around my shoulders like a warm blanket. I remember thinking, "This is God's hug."

I had the same feeling years later as an adult when, for the first time, I wrapped a prayer shawl around me and I felt myself wrapped in God's presence.

There is holiness in I-thou encounters with people. I have felt God's presence in encounters with the frail, the ill, the impaired, the dying. Not all the time of course, but often enough to know that my work sometimes opens those entrances to holiness.

For example, as I left from my last visit with a dying woman, she said, "God bless you." Her words, her prayer, opened one of those entrances to holiness. God's presence filled the room, and I felt blessed.

Another time, I, a Jewish chaplain, was called to the room of a large, close-knit Italian family whose father had just died. They were awaiting the arrival of their youngest daughter Cathy, whom they described as a severely disturbed schizophrenic who was a born again Christian fundamentalist. She had been very close to her father, and the family was worried about her reaction to his death. When she arrived, the family asked for a prayer, and we formed a circle around her father's bed. I had been told that Cathy didn't like to be touched by strangers, so I was surprised when she took my hand to complete the circle. In a moment of Divine inspiration, I asked her to say the prayer. I don't remember her words, but I know that I witnessed a moment of wholeness in her brokenness. And the moment was holy.

Lawrence Kushner is right. Entrances to holiness are everywhere! We can't make miracles happen, but sometimes if we slow our pace and open our eyes and our hearts, we may become aware of the moments of holiness that surround us.

Life is a pilgrimage towards holiness. I hope these reflections aid you on your spiritual journey.